I0532999

The Adventures of Jason and Bo
"It's good to be different"

By Alistair Harden
Illustrated by Kristine Bizzarro

The Adventures of Jason and Bo

"It's good to be different"

Copyright ©2013 by Alistair Harden

Illustrations and cover painting ©2013 by Kristine Bizzarro

Published by:
Alaska Dreams Publishing
www.alaskadp.com

Revision 20140222

ISBN numbers:
ISBN-13: 978-0-9855588-5-7
ISBN-10: 0985558857
E-Book versions available.
See the website at **www.alaskadp.com** for links.

Table of Contents

Dedication

To the Gwich'in Athabaskan Indians of northeast Alaska and northwest Canada, they have shared their land, their food, their stories and their lives with me. I would like to dedicate this book to the young of their nation and to Jacob Wright and his sons. May you always take pride in your heritage, yourself, and your history. The members of that nation that I have met truly are "The People of the Land" and have been for over 20,000 years.

Acknowledgements

To my beloved wife and the illustrator of my visions, thank you for all your support, hard work and belief in this project. You had faith in me and encouraged me throughout the whole process. This book would not be the book it is today without your undying support and continued works.

Chapter One

There are short people, heavy people, tall people, and thin people. They come in all shades of color: brown, white, yellow, darker shades and lighter shades. All these people can make the world a better place to live in. Some of them grow up in a family with only one parent, some kids live with just their mother, and other kids live with only their father. The boy in our story Jason happens to live with his father and grandfather. They live in Big Bull, Alaska. It's a small town nestled at the bottom of a snow covered mountain called Beaver Kill. There is only one road in and out of Big Bull. The glacial fed Black River runs along the left side of town, its surging currents pouring out into the emerald blue pacific. On the other side is the towering Beaver Kill. The town sits in between these two mighty creations on a rocky strip of land about a mile wide. Another thing that surrounds the town is a great boreal forest that stretches out for hundreds of miles, with thick groves of ancient spruce and shimmering aspen, Paper Birch and knotted Willow. This is an Alaskan logging town. Life isn't always easy in this rugged land; the town can get blocked by spring floods and winter snows, even avalanches, sometimes for days or weeks. It is at those times that the people of the town must come together and help each other. They band together like a big family and they make sure everyone is taken care of, even if they may not look the same or talk the same.

Mr. Frank is the local logging foreman and Jason's father. He is a big man, standing over six feet tall and wears a red plaid jacket with big black buttons on the front and a wide black collar. He keeps that collar always turned up against the wind. His heavy wool pants smell of spruce trees and chainsaw gas. With dark brown eyes and coal black hair he has a powerful presence, but in his eyes a person can see stress and years of worry. It seems he always has problems on his mind. Those problems show in the lines on his forehead and the taut way in which he holds his mouth. You see, after Jason's mother moved away Mr. Frank had to work more and more. There were always things the family needed and bills to pay so Mr. Frank was gone a lot; that left Jason mostly in the care of his grandfather.

Jason loves his PaPaw, for that's what he calls him. PaPaw and Jason spend hours and sometimes whole days in the woods sleeping out under the stars on nice nights or building a shelter of branches and moss when it rains. Sometimes they even sleep in snow caves they dig themselves to sleep warm on winter nights. It was there, under the big round spruce trees, sitting outside in the woods on the cool earth that Jason had learned many of "The Old Ways"….

Papaw had told him, "I have tried to teach these lessons to your father, but he has never really wanted to learn our ways. He always seemed drawn to the world outside, to the outsider ways". I don't blame your father; he grew up very fast and did the best he could do". Jason would often think about things like this, about how he was different from most of the other people in town. Sometimes the kids at school would say things and tease him about being different. Sometimes he could not think about these things, about being different, but often it would bother him and he would wish all the world was the same, that all men were from the same place and spoke the same way…. ate the same foods, knew the same lessons and told the same stories.

Jason thought to himself that if everyone was the same it would solve many of the problems he has seen.

When those times of thinking would come he would go find his dog, Bo. Bo was always happy to see him and would wag his big white tail and talk with him through his soft blue eyes. It seemed to Jason, that Bo was the best Husky any boy could ever have for his own. Bo never cared what anyone looked like or where they came from. He would walk in the woods or down to the store with Jason. Sometimes they would lie together on the grass and watch the clouds drift by or chase birds down on the beach. Bo was Jason's only friend.

Bo had such a beautiful, warm coat of black and white. That coat could even keep Jason warm when they camped out at Rosen's North Star Mine. The mine sat halfway up Beaver Kill Mountain and was once the biggest mining operation for hundreds of miles. It began in the early 1900's and there are endless tunnels and mine shafts all over the big mountain. The tunnels are the scars from where hard men stripped it from within for its precious rock. Jason knew how dangerous an abandoned mine shaft was. He was always careful and trusted the word of his father and grandfather to stay away. It was up on Beaver Kill mountain overlooking the Hard Tree Valley and the swift flowing water of Black River that Jason loved to camp. He often went up there to be alone and look for moose and bear. He would stay away from the mine entrance and camp out front on the flat part of the wide ledge, eat wild game like black duck soup and caribou sausage . He set his camp so it over looked that raw, wild valley and the cascading water fall of the Black River. He would even camp up there in the fall and early winter. The water fall would freeze in the winter and create a giant frozen ice sculpture. When the boy stayed up there then, the unmoving falls seemed like it was frozen in time to him.

Chapter Two:

Shelly and Mrs. Harkin

Monday was not Jason's favorite day. His father Mr. Frank would get up early on weekdays and start a fire in the wood cook stove. Jason would often stay in bed as long as he could, waiting for the heat from the fire to warm up their cabin. He would lie in his bed with the blankets pulled up to his cold nose and watch his breath turn to steam in his room. There was a faint light coming from the kitchen. Just outside his door he heard Papaw cough in the other room. His grandfather had not looked well last night and hearing his cough made Jason wonder if he had caught a flu bug. His grandfather was a tough man, but he was getting close to seeing 75 winters now. From bed Jason could only hear mumbled voices that would wake him when the two old men talked in the kitchen.

Then he would hear the sizzle of food. The smells of breakfast would waft into his room and hit his nose. His tummy would growl for breakfast. With a groan Jason would throw the covers back, slip his feet into his boots and clomp, clomp, clomp over to the warm stove. He'd hastily try and wrestle a blanket over his shoulders to keep the cold from his skin. His dad would open the fridge door, grab an old Mason jar off the counter and pour him a glass of juice. Slowly with trembling hands, his body shivering to stay warm, Jason would reach out, take the jar and push the glass up to his lips, letting the cold juice quench his morning thirst.

While the conversation often revolved around work for the day, old hunting stories or family gossip, he really liked sitting in the cabin warmed by the fire, talking with father and grandfather. He wished he could sit and talk with them for hours and hours, but Jason knew it would soon be over and his PaPaw would be saying, "Hurry up you're gonna be late". It was that time again, fall had come and the cool weather meant it was time to get ready for school and for winter. School had started two weeks before, but this morning Jason took the time and found his winter gear before heading out - knowing he would need them soon. Putting on his gloves, his favorite wool coat and topping his head with a cap, he was off. Jason went out the door and headed up the street dragging his now booted feet. Not really in a great rush to get there; hands covered in fur lined gloves and carrying all his school supplies on his back he strode up the rutted dirt road, nudging his way to the small yellow building. Always in September Mrs. Harkin would be waiting. After a summer of camping, hiking and fishing it was time to go back to his studies.

Mrs. Harkin had been teaching at the school since Jason's father had gone there. Through the years she had become the assistant principle and now the principle. She was a very strong woman, known all over town for her skill in cribbage. Every man in town also knew she was a woman you couldn't out-argue.

Her hair had grown gray with the years, but some of the young blonde woman would show through from time to time. Although a very proper woman, she had realized long ago the uselessness of dresses, skirts, and ladies shoes in Big Bull Alaska. Now she wore what only made sense to Jason; a clean pair of blue jeans, a heavy shirt of plaid or chamois and pack boots. She would change her boots for tennis shoes while she was indoors. Outside in those pack boots, walking toward you on the school yard, with a yellow light from the street lamp behind her, her face hid in shadows, all you could see was the bulk of clothes and the bent of her head as she powered toward you…. "Man she looks big….and mean" was all Jason could think.

There were lots of children in Big Bull Elementary School, but many of them seemed very different to Jason, especially Shelly Johnson. Her father owned the logging company and was Mr. Frank's boss. It seemed to Jason that Shelly had everything in the world. Both her parents lived together with her on High Street at the end of town. They all lived in a huge two story house with lots of windows and bright lights always shined from it. At Christmas the big blue house with the red door was decorated with tons of colored lights. Shelly had nice clothes, new boots, and toys.

She seemed to know everyone in school. With her long yellow hair, her white skin and deep blue eyes, Jason could hardly think how she would ever want for anything. Her life was perfect and she would never be scared or know hunger. She was so very different from him.

Her life was different, always talking of stupid things and she knew about books and art. She liked fancy store bought clothes and she smelled of flowers. She had no reason to act bad towards him. He could be mad at her, but he knew it was not her fault. Even when she was being mean to him and he wanted to yell at her, to tell her how good her life was and that she had no reason to be mean, he wouldn't. He would just think about Bo, close his ears and walk away.

On this Monday Jason had heard of the early snow storm as it was announced on the radio. He had heard of it while eating breakfast with his family. The news of storms never bothered him. Not even a surprise September one. There is always blowing wind, snow and cold during the school year in Alaska. Looking out the window as he sat at his desk, Jason would drift away in thought and watch the windblown snow cross the frosted glass.

Invading the class room Mrs. Harkin announced, "This storm is getting worse. I have talked with the School Superintendent and the Weather Service and I have decided that early release is the best course of action". All at once every student in the classroom yelled, "YIPPEE"!! The loud shouts of joy shook him from his day dreaming. Even Jason was happy to have a short school day. Knowing PaPaw had not been feeling well he thought today would be a good day to stay home and take care of his grandfather.

The weather was getting pretty bad, so sitting with PaPaw and listening to his stories would be a good way to spend the rest of his day.

Jason and the other kids were hurrying to their lockers, grabbing coats and hats and talking excitedly about having the day off. The noise was growing very loud while Mrs. Harkin and Jason's teacher were funneling the kids out the door. In the background you could hear, "Now don't dawdle, you children go right home. I have phoned your parents and they are expecting you. Hurry now children, hurry"!

While holding the door open both of the adults were counting kids to make sure they all were out. Jason was right behind Shelly and a couple other kids as everyone left. He was very close and trying to pass them on the path outside the school. The snow was making it hard for him to look forward. Trying to push them from behind, "Jeez"!! he thought to himself, "Hurry up". He was in a hurry to get back to the cabin, pet Bo and talk with his grandfather. About half way down the path Jason heard Shelly say, "Oh, my gosh! My new hat, I forgot my new hat. I must go back and get it". Jason pushed by the other kids as Shelly turned and started back up the path towards the school.

Alistair Harden

Chapter Three

Shelly's Walk Home

It was getting cold and Shelly was mad at herself for forgetting the new hat. Mom had bought it on her parent's last trip into Anchorage. It was very soft with light blue trim and it was so white. Shelly new her mother would be mad if she lost it. Pulling on the heavy school door she stepped inside. Noticing how dark it was she stopped. Light from the outside street lamp was shining down the tile floor and the shadows made the lockers look like big, grey guards lining the hallway. Just as the door was closing the street lights began to flicker. Shelly hurried, sensing the storm had grown very bad. The snow was now coming down in heavy sheets of white, the wind groaning as it pushed the heavy snow around. Shelly ran down the hall and grabbed her hat. Throwing open her classroom door, she ran out into the hallway toward the exit. With one last flicker, all was dark. "Oh Dear" she thought, "Oh Dear, what shall I do"?

Standing motionless in the middle of the hall, peering into the darkness she forced her eyes to see, waiting patiently for them to adjust to the lack of light. Taking a big deep breath, Shelly thought to herself, the path leads right on to High Street and I can still see enough to follow the path to High Street and then follow High Street home. Feeling her way she moved slowly down the hallway until she felt the crossbar of the door. Pushing at the exit door, its heavy steel pushing back she could tell the wind had grown stronger and colder. She squeezed by the door, letting it go, and it closed behind her with a Bang! Holding onto the stair rail she started down the snow covered stairs. The snow pelting against her cheeks in stickle blasts. Once at the bottom Shelly continued down the path. It was about halfway to where she had just turned around when Shelly thought to herself, "Where did the path go"? The wind was blowing so hard now and the snow was coming down so fast, but Shelly kept moving forward. Pulling her new hat down over her ears and slipping her hands in her coat pockets she walked forward. Shelly was sure High Street was right in front of her.

She kept waiting to see High Street or the edge of the sidewalk, but it was not there. She slowly walked on and on but it was getting real dark now. Turning around she could not see anything. There was no path, no school, no lights, no High Street. Shelly felt a deep fear come over her and was, in an instant, very scared.

Jason had made it home and now sat in the light of the oil lamps talking with his grandfather. Papaw looked very hot; he was red and sweating a lot. Trying to make him feel better Jason talked of big bulls and black duck soup. He was telling him how he was getting old enough now to go out with his grandfather on hunts. Papaw was nodding his head in agreement when they heard a knock at the door. Jason looked at his grandfather. Papaw looked towards the door and raised his chin, so Jason got up and walked over to the door. Knock, knock, "Hello, Hello"? It was Mrs. Harkin. "What is she doing here"? He thought. "Didn't she know there was a storm blowing out there"? Jason stepped back and let Mrs. Harkin in. As she entered, white swirling snow came in with her, wrapping around her feet like an old cat.

Mrs. Harkin went straight to Jason's grandfather and began to tell him of a missing girl. "Missing Girl"! Jason thought. He got concerned, "Who is missing?" he asked. Mrs. Harkin turned to face him and with a furled forehead and worried eyes said, "Shelly." "Shelly"! Cried Jason. "I saw her when we left school. I was right behind her. She had got halfway down the school walk when I overheard her say she had to go back to get her hat. She went back to the school"

"We have already looked through the whole school", said Mrs. Harkin. "She just isn't there".

Mrs. Harkin again turned to Jason's Grandfather and was asking him if he could help. Everyone knew the old man was the best tracker in the area. Jason thought, "There isn't anyone better in the whole of Alaska". If anyone could find Shelly in a storm it would be his Papaw. As Jason's grandfather tried to get up he started to cough and wheeze. He tried to force himself up and out of bed but he fell back down. The flu was getting worse and Jason could see there was no way the old man would make it out to find Shelly. Not in this storm.

Waving his hand Papaw summoned the boy to his bedside. In a hushed voice he asked, "Do you remember the lessons I taught you, about how to track in a storm"? Do you remember how snow drifts in the wind but changes as a person walks through it? Do you think you can find her"?

The old man was staring into his eyes. Jason stammered, thinking he could, but he was still young and this is grown-up stuff. His grandfather put both hands on Jason's shoulders and squeezed. In a slow, strong voice he said, "This is very important Jason, Shelly will not survive the night. Remember the lessons I have taught you. I can't go. Your father never learned our ways. The other men are looking all over town, but they don't know what you know. Do you understand? You take Bo, go back to the school, look for her path and find her, Ok? It's up to you grandson. You are the only one". Jason's heart was beating so fast. He looked at his grandfather and said "Yes. Yes grandfather I'll find her".

Bo, sensing the tension in the room stood up, stretched and with a big yawn walked over to Jason.

Looking up at him and wagging his tail, Bo rested his side against Jason's leg waiting for a pat.

Jason looked down at his friend and said, "Ok Bo, it looks like it's up to us. Are you ready boy"?

Chapter Four

Jason and Bo Head Out

The wind was rushing past as Jason opened the door. Bo brushed by him and bounded out into the mound of snow that his front yard had become. It had taken some time to get ready. His grandfather was telling him things to get and tools to remember as he stuffed his pack and checked his clothes and his supplies. Mrs. Harkin helped him get all his gear together and told Jason she would stay so he wouldn't worry about his Grandfather. Papaw mentioned to her that perhaps she should try and find Jason's Dad and let him know what was happening. She agreed and left as Jason was pulling on his coat. Promising to return right away, she quickly opened the cabin door, braced against the storm, lit her flashlight and disappeared behind a wall of blowing snow.

Stepping outside Jason bent down and called for Bo.

He came bouncing over, tail held high, and sat in front of the Jason. Reaching out with both arms, Jason hugged his neck and cleared his throat. "Bo", he said. "All the men are searching down towards High Street and around the school.

Let's go take a look and see what we think". With Bo leaping back and forth he strode into the tempest.

In his big fur mittens Jason held tight to a long flashlight. He had packed extra batteries and even a smaller flashlight. In this storm the dark was not his friend, but even with his big bright Mag-light Jason would have to swing his flashlight from building to building. In this snow storm it helped him to keep in a straight line. Bo had no such problems. Somehow he knew where Jason wanted to go and plowed through the drifts towards the small yellow school house. Jason stopped at the bottom of the walk and could see lots of sign where men, women and kids had passed while looking for Shelly. Where to look with all these tracks and signs of people everywhere? How would he find where Shelly had gone? Bigger circles!!

That is what his grandfather had taught him. Papaw had said, "If you lost the trail, or the track crossed lots of other tracks you needed to stop, then move out and circle the place where you last saw sign, and then move away a bit more and circle again. So this is what Jason and Bo did. They kept circling and circling and moving away, stepping out in ever growing loops. Soon the tracks got further and further apart. There was less sign in the snow now. Bo with his nose down and Jason with his flashlight sweeping in one long beam broken only by the blowing snow, they searched for her tracks.

Enough time had passed and the snow had blown away any real tracks. What Jason was looking for was more of a depression. Like laying a log in sand or a trail where a giant had dragged a bag. That was all he was going to have after such a long time. His mind thought of Shelly, of how different and how unprepared she was. Jason knew if you were lost in a storm to stop and dig a hole in a snow-bank. You could crawl inside and, even without a candle or a way to make heat, your body would soon warm that hole and it would keep the wind off you.

He knew the wind could steal heat from his body. He knew then that his mind would slow down and his thinking would get confused, and after a time his body would slow until he froze. Jason also knew Shelly didn't know any of that.

Jason kept circling just as Papaw had shown him many times. He found that long low curl in the snow. There were no other tracks around and no other sign, but he could see it clearly. He knew Shelly had crossed the road and was headed right towards Beaver Kill. Jason was about four hundred yards down the trail. However, with the lights out and the town dark he didn't really know if he was four hundred yards or four hundred feet from where he had crossed the road.

He followed her trail into the woods shining his light, moving it back-n-forth across the low curl and started up the Rosen's Mine trail. He followed her sign and saw a place in the snow where Shelly had stopped under the branches of an ancient spruce. Jason also saw something else and he stopped. Bo stopped too, and then the hair on the dog's back straightened, reaching into the air, a low growl coming from his throat. Jason knew as Bo did, that a bear had also found the girls trail. Shelly and the beast had made good sign once they were in the woods and Jason realized why Shelly had stopped. As soon as she got to the tree line she must have either seen or heard the bear. Often, frightened people will get themselves into more trouble. Fear takes over and they do not always react in a thoughtful way. Without thinking she must have run. Run up the trail, away from the safety and warmth of town.

Jason was right.

Alistair Harden

Chapter Five

Shelly and the Beast

In long, lingering gasps Shelly was trying to breathe. Her breath was coming heavy on her chest as she pushed her body to go further. The bear had come at her out of the storm like a great ship emerging from a fog, its massive head swaying from side to side. The bear was moving towards her in long easy strides.

Shelly held back a scream, her heart pulsing with fear. She fought to stay in control, fought to think. She had to keep the panic down in her belly and not let it rise up and consume her mind. Shelly knew instinctively that the bear had not seen her, but was tracking her by smell. She tore off her hat and threw it to the ground and began to run. Shelly had been taught to never run from a bear. But in this case she knew it was better to run, and by throwing her hat down she also knew the bear would stop and sniff her hat. That gave her extra time to get as far away from the bear as she could. In a panicked tramp she ran without a destination in mind. All she could think was to run. The snow was knee deep and running almost impossible, her gate was more of a push. Pushing snow with her thighs she struggled forward.

Her mind was a blur and her legs screamed in pain. The young girl was driven by sheer terror and adrenaline. She was crashing through brush and getting hit in face with branches. Small cuts from the forest's frozen garden had drawn blood. Each branch and bush froze hard in the storm had steel-like edges and left their mark on her skin. Feeling warm blood drip down her face, being forced deeper into the woods, her mind was awhirl with thoughts of dread. The ground rose up before her. Willing herself uphill she moved deeper into the forbidding dark. Now each step came slower and tighter, as even her spirit seemed exhausted. Finally not able to go a step further she reached out and put her hands on an old rotting stump. Shelly's head hung low and her body was rising and falling with her struggling breaths. She picked her head up and looked around. Her wet hair hung down over her face and she brushed it away from her eyes, fearing she would see the menace stalking her. This was it. Stopping only for as long as it took for the pain to leave her muscles and her lungs to gulp air, she pushed off of the rough bark with a shove, focusing up the mountain and began again.

The storm was not so bad now, and through the trees Shelly noticed a light glow. The clouds were breaking up and the moonlight began to break through the dark spruce forest. Trees began to take shape and the trail was easier to see. Shelly was still pushing hard up the mountain when she saw a dark shape; it seemed darker than everything else and above it a brown form. It was a sign. As she got closer she could make out old faded letters. The sign read, "Rosen's North Star Mine".

She reached a big flat area with steep rocks along the back side. To her right, along with the dark spot and that old board was a wall of stone. As the wind died down she could hear water. The moonlight showed her that off to her left was a steep cliff and the water falls that went to the valley floor below. Down there was the Black Water River. Then she realized to her horror, that this was a dead end. There was only one way out, the way she had come. And the bear was coming up the trail behind her.

Chapter Six

Jason and Bo on the Trail

Jason and Bo could sense they were close and Jason knew exactly where Shelly was now. There was only one place that a person could walk to in this area of the mountain. He knew it well. Jason pressed hard through the snow but kept a sharp look out for the bear. Bo was stalking along beside him with a muffled grumble in his belly. Oh how he hoped Shelly was okay. They turned a corner on the path and there he was, the big bear standing in the trail with his head down, blocking the way. It looked like he was sniffing at something. On all fours his back was above Jason's shoulders. With well-rounded ears and a long nose this was a male bear. Jason could see long strings of white dripping from his mouth. Curling his lips, the bear inhaled the girl's scent. Jason grabbed Bo and began a silent retreat. He stepped back and hoped to get behind a giant spruce. He had taken just two steps back when all at once the wind changed. Soon the bear sniffed, instantly alert, he stood up and caught the smell of man and dog. His massive brown body stood like a great tree. His nose was raised high in the air and he poked it in each direction trying to locate the pair. With a thud he came off his hind legs and slammed his body onto all fours. Looking in the direction of the scent the bear saw the two of them standing no more than 40 yards away. Enraged, the bear stared and took one step. He stopped, still sniffing; he winded them and took another slow, cat-like prowling step. Winding them again, with a snarl, it let out a loud ROAR! Hunching up on all fours the beast's muscles straining for release. In an instant flash it exploded. Coming at them with an audible "Guff", snapping its jaws and staying low, like a brown flat train, the bear charged.

Snow moved away from its large body like waves away from a boat, powerful shoulders and claws digging into the frozen ground, gaining speed. Bo jumped out in front of Jason growling and barking. The big Husky stood between the wild creature coming fast, and Jason. Then Bo charged and with wild screams and howls he ran at the bear. The bear stopped and the two stood nose to nose, their breath billowing up between them, eyes wild and teeth bared they circled each other in the snow.

The dog's hair was standing straight up and bristling with contempt. Glimpsing at his Jason over his shoulder to confirm his place of protection, Bo would lunge and the great beast would jump back. The bear was swatting and roaring. The dog jumped in low and fast, snapping back. Each animal took turns lunging and retreating as they circled each other, trying to sniff out a weakness or an advantage. Jason wasn't sure what he could do. He was scared Bo would get hurt, but was lost as to how he could help. Papaw's voice in his head broke the moment. He heard, "Jason use the whistle in your pack".... The whistle, of course!! He knew that loud noises scared bears. He had been taught this from the time he was a young child. Jason quickly removed his pack. He was watching the two brutes still circling and jousting for position. Brushing aside a piece of wrapped moose meat he dug quickly into his gear and found his whistle. He brought it up to his teeth, clenched it firmly. He squinted and focused on the fight, he was timing his move. As Bo moved around to his front, Jason ran towards the pair; blowing as hard as he could on that whistle and waving his arms. The bear was stunned. Between Bo snapping and barking, the whistle's shrill piercing the night and this other thing waving its arms and running at him, it was just too much. The great beast broke. It turned and with a jump ran off the trail and downhill, his massive body thundering and shuddering away through the dense, black forest.

Chapter Seven

The Journey Home

Shelly had heard a sound; there was something on the wind. She strained to hear the noise, but was she was shivering so hard that her teeth chattered against each other and cold, brittle, thin layers of ice seemed to form down her back. The bear, the bear. She was thinking of the animal - it must be close now. Her hat gone, she was frightened, exhausted and just wanted to be home. She was remembering her nice warm house with her mother and father, the warm glow of the many lights that covered their home. Shelly bent down on her knees with her arms crossed in front of her. Matted hair fell into her hands and sweat mixed with drops of blood that landed in the snow at her feet. Crying, alone and terrified, Shelly wanted to give up. She wanted to stop moving. This was way outside anything she had known. The woods, wild animals, the weather, it was all so horrible, like a nightmare that wouldn't end. With a quick snap, she stood up. Reaching down within herself she gathered her mind and her strength. Getting a hold of herself from a place deep within, she found courage and made herself stand. That bear was not gonna get her. Shelly slowly backed towards the black hole in the cliff. She moved toward the brown sign with its faded letters and was getting ready to run down into the mine. If that bear wanted her she wasn't going to make it easy.

As she began to turn an animal leaped from the shadows. Her heart jumped and she began to scream and spinning around she turned to run. Then she heard a voice, "Wait! Shelly stop"! Looking over her shoulder she moved forward. Her mind still clouded from fear and adrenaline. It took a moment for her to realize it wasn't the bear; she looked harder through the moonlit shadows. A boy and a dog!? She couldn't believe what she was seeing. "I know this boy" she thought, and it came to her, "Jason, Bo is that you"? Jason walked up to her with a big smile and kind brown eyes. He walked up panting and said, "I found you". He pulled the load from his back and Bo nosed into Shelly's leg and sat looking up at her with those soft blue eyes.

Pulling her a dry warm coat from his pack, he handed it to her, "You really should put this on," he said. Jason then bent down on one knee and took out his fire starting kit. He grabbed some small twigs and a few branches, and his well-practiced hands soon had a fire going. Sitting close to the high rocky wall behind them they were sheltered from the winds, and the heat of the fire reflected off the rock wall surface. In a matter of minutes Shelly stopped shaking and began to dry out her wet clothes by the heat of the fire. Jason looked at her and turned to his backpack; he took out some water from a white plastic canteen, along with a soft cotton cloth. He wetted the cloth and gently began to clean her cuts. He smiled his big broad smile to reassure her it would be okay. The cold water began to reduce the swollen flesh and it felt good on her face. He then reached down and took her hands in his. He turned them over and looked at them. Her hands were dirty, but they were okay. So he cleaned them. Grabbing a towel from the same bag he handed it to her, moving slowly so as not to frighten her further. As she dried her face and hands Jason finished checking her further for any other injuries.

Jason took some food from his pack and gave Shelly a thermos of hot tea and a tin cup. She was so thankful for Jason. He had saved her from a terrible night. She was sure he had saved her life. She was warm and had food and tea to drink, she felt safe. Bo wagging his tail and asking for a treat with his eyes, she knew he would protect them and warn them should the need arise. Thinking of how different her life was from Jason's she realized that without Jason she may never have seen her mother or father again. She realized that it was because he was different and lived in a different way that he was able to find her, chase off the bear, warm her and make her feel safe. She felt ashamed for thinking and saying all those mean things to him just because he was different from her. He was not like a lot of the other children, but she slowly began to realize it was good that Jason was different, and she was glad he was who he was.

She was deep in her thoughtful reflection when Jason put a hand on her shoulder and gave her some warm meat he had been roasting over the fire. The smell of the grease dripping onto the red hot coals made her mouth water with hunger. She snatched it from him and tore into it. Letting out a "Mmm", she laid her head back against the ledge and chewed the hot moose brisket, the warm meat satisfying her hunger. She took long swallows of water between bites and replenished her dehydrated body. After a while with the fire dying down and Shelly having regained her strength, they all began their journey home. Bo was out front leading the way, his tail held high. Shelly and Jason talked about their families and their lives as they descended down off the mountain. They chatted while he watched her steps closely and kept a skillful eye on her. If she stumbled and fell now it would be hours getting her out of the woods and Jason wanted to get her home quickly. They soon found out that, although they were different from each other in many ways, they were also very much the same. They both even talked about their common dislike of Cream of Wheat, ech! They laughed about the food in the lunch room and how the older people just didn't understand how kids are.

The more they talked the more they became friends. Jason also woke up to the fact that Shelly may have more things in her life, more toys maybe, or better clothes, but without a grandfather like his. She was missing many things that Jason took for granted in his own life. Jason learned to walk in the ways of the wild. He knew how to survive in a world very different from the one Shelly came from. He was smiling as he thought on these things. With Shelly's traveling voice in his ears he felt his heart swell with a very strange feeling. It was a good feeling, a feeling he had never really felt before. He was happy to be who he was, he was proud of his family and of the ways of his people. Jason was proud to be different.

Alistair Harden

Chapter Eight

Lessons Learned

When the three new friends got to the trail entrance and looked out across the meadow they could see that the lights of the town had come back on. Jason flashed his light towards the road and soon heard muffled calls. There were grown-ups all over and lights flashing up and down the streets. The houses seemed as bright as the sun. Shelly quickened her pace. Jason and Bo followed behind. There, standing across High Street Shelly saw her mother and father.

They ran towards each other, her father scooping her up, crying. With tears of joy they embraced. Mr. Frank was there too. He was smiling and looking at his son. He strode over, hugged the boy and slapped him gently on the shoulder while saying, "You should be proud of yourself son. You found Shelly and brought all of you home safe". Shelly's father walked over and shook Jason's hand, pumping it up and down he thanked the boy over and over again then reached down and scratched behind Bo's ears.

Shelly's father was laughing from deep down in his belly. He smiled and even gave Mr. Frank a hug. With his teeth shining in the moonlight and a big smile on his face he said, "I'll never be able to thank you enough". A crowd was gathering as the news about the kid's return spread. From all over town people moved out of houses and down streets, making their way down to the trio to welcome them home. Then he turned and in a loud voice announced, "Everyone please give a cheer for Jason and his dog Bo. They are true heroes and have brought my daughter back to me". Hip, Hip Hurrah, Hip, Hip Hurrah. All the adults and even the kids that were out in the street were cheering for Jason and Bo.

It was very late when the crowd started to thin out and, with thankful hearts the town's people went back to their homes. Jason couldn't wait to get back to his grandfather and tell him of his adventure. Jason hurried home with his father behind him. He walked through the gate, ran up the front steps of the long covered porch and pushed open the cabin door. With his chest full of pride he moved to his grandfather's bedside a bright twinkle in his eyes. Bending down he put his hand on his grandfather's shoulder. Slowly the old man turned and smiled up at him, patting the back of Jason's hand, a small tear on his cheek. "I did it grandfather. Papaw, I did as you asked. I saved her". The old man smiled, grabbed Jason and brought him in close. With a strong hug from arms strengthened by a life in the woods he said, "I am so proud of you, Jason. You were the only one that could save that girl. Be proud of yourself".

Things would always be very different for Jason. When he went back to school he was invited to sit with the other kids. He was happy and proud. Shelly would smile at him and make it a point to talk with him. She often asked him to walk her home after school. They would talk about that night and about the bear. They laughed and smiled together and became good friends.

With Bo at his side Jason moved up High Street and smiled at the world. He was glad now that people were different, that everyone has talents and gifts to share. He thought about how wrong he had been when he wanted the whole world to be the same. He thought how dull and boring it would be if everyone looked the same, ate the same food and knew the same stories. Jason was proud that everyone was different, but also the same.

THE END

If you enjoyed this story, please consider posting a review. Thank you!

■■

The following chapter is an excerpt from the next book in The Adventures of Jason and Bo series.

If you'd like to be notified when the next book in the Jason and Bo series is released, please sign up for the ADP mailing list at:

http://www.alaskadp.com/signup.html

■■

Doing it Right - Excerpt

The Adventures of Jason and Bo

Chapter One

The noise of the plane's engine was so loud it was roaring and Jason couldn't hear what the pilot was saying. The wash from the prop was blowing his long black hair into his eyes as he tried to locate the planes foot step. He had passed his pack and gear up to the pilot and it was secure. Now it was his turn to get up into the yellow and white machine. The wind from the prop was weaving over Bo's long fur. Standing on the step, using just his hands to motion, he told Bo to "Load up". The big Husky jumped into the Cessna 172 and then into the back. The single engine plane was taking them up to the Good News River to meet his Pawpaw. The Good News is located in the Kuskokwim River Drainage in Southwest Alaska. The Kuskokwim River provides the principle drainage for the remote Alaska Interior on the west side of the Alaska Range of mountains. Its towering white mountains, covered most of the year in snow, send torrents of water down the slopes and into the rivers as they flow southwest towards Kuskokwim Bay. The Kuskokwim is broad and flat, it is not an area he and Grandfather traditionally fished, but Pawpaw had been invited by an old Yupik friend and he asked Jason if he wanted to go. Jason had met Umagak once before on a Caribou hunt up on the Kobuk. It was on that hunt that he had his first 'Shee Fish', while hunting the broad, wet valleys along the plains and foothills of the Brooks Range. The man he remembered was quiet and content. His wide nose perched above thin lips. When he smiled it was big and happy. The old Yupik didn't let the fact that his two front teeth were missing diminish his smile. He had almond shaped eyes that peered out from the fur trimmed hood of his old worn parka. At night they had sat at the fire and Umagak told Jason about the land he was now flying into. He couldn't believe it, his excitement was still buzzing inside his body like a bee in a can.

The Kuskokwim translates into 'Slow Moving Thing', in the Yupik language and Jason's thoughts drifted again to what it would be like standing in that wide river casting his lines and concentrating on how to move his fly or lure to hook the big one.

Jason buckled himself in the passenger seat next to the pilot, grabbed the headset and put it on.

The headset blocked out most of the engine noise and through it he could hear the pilot, "Hi my name is Bill, Bill Guffstuvsin". Jason reached out and shook the big blond man's hand. "Are you ready, son"? Bill asked with a big smile.

Jason nodded his head up and down real fast, as excited as he was, his big brown eyes wide and bright. "This is going to be awesome", he thought to himself. The pilot pulled down on the bill of his baseball cap, gave Jason a wink, and pushed the throttle foreword. The engine began to rev while he stood on the breaks. Soon the little single engine began to whine under the stress. Like an Alaskan sled dog held back on rope, the four seater began to lunge and jump. When the rpm's on the motor hit the red-line on the indicator, the pilot let off the breaks and Jason was pushed back into his seat as the plane shot down the runway. Jason was really wound-up and Bo was watching him real close, he could sense his friend was thrilled. Looking out the windows the trees began to blur by in a rush and soon Jason felt his stomach fall as the little Cessna lifted off the ground then began to climb towards the northeast.

From where he sat the trees became a muddled green brown and he could watch the Black River snake its way from Beaver Kill Mountain down to the Pacific Ocean.

This was Jason's first flight and he was soaking in every moment, every vibration of the plane and every sight he could see. He was flying! He couldn't believe it, flying!! Up in the broken white clouds they flew along the Pacific's mountainous coast. There were waterfalls cascading down the deep, green mountainsides. The icy blue glaciers forced their way between the glassy peaks, as they crept down to the ocean. A white line formed at the place where water and land met. Down there the ocean was dark and he could make out the white tops as waves broke over in the wind.

Still looking out the window he thought about all the fish he was going to catch. He thought about the beautiful spotted Dolly Varden trout he could find in the fast flowing waters. The Arctic Grayling with its sail-like dorsal fin and its rich dark coloring, the amazing Shee fish wearing silvery sides, darkening to blackish-green along top and the large silver scales. Shee Fish was Jason's favorite and he liked it better than Halibut, even though they were kinda the same.

The boy had spent the previous couple of days reading over the fishing regulations for this new area. His Grandfather had taught him to respect the fish and game laws of Alaska. He was told that they are there to protect the land and the animals so his children, and his children's children would always enjoy the bounty of this great land. Jason had memorized how many of each fish he could catch in a day and just what sizes were legal. He had spent hours going over his fishing gear and putting new line on his reels. He organized his fishing box and cleaned his lures. Grandfather had taken the food and the tent with him and had left a day early to set up camp, as Jason had school to finish.

Reaching back behind his seat he strained to grab his day-pack. Clamping down with his right hand he took hold of it and set the pack on his lap. Taking out his maps, he went over his mental notes as he again was carefully studying the area around the Good News River. In his mind he could smell the fresh air and see the wide-open vistas. They came to life as he looked down on the green USGS map. It was a wild place, he could tell. Well preserved; nature as it was in the beginning. He knew there would not be a lot of people around but he was hoping some kids his age would be there. He had a feeling the fishing was going to be epic.

Imagine having the whole area to himself? The creeks and sloughs, the sandy spits and deep water river eddies. What a fishing trip this was going to be! He could hardly sit in his seat. In his research of the river the boy had learned that each season begins with an incredible return of the largest of all the Salmon, the mighty King. The fish have not come back like they used to in other places in Interior Alaska. His grandfather had told him how over fishing and pollution were driving down the Salmon returns, but the Good News has had some of its strongest returns in history. This is why Pawpaw's friend Umagak had invited them to fish. The Elder Yupik had learned of problems others were having filling their smoke houses and freezers for the long Alaskan winters. It has been more than two years now and the Kings still had not returned in those areas like they used to.

From the map, it looked like an ideal river to take a King Salmon. Jason thought he would try to take one with a fly. He could see the smile on his grandfather's face and imagined the light in his eyes as Jason held up the great fish for him to admire. He also had read how Chums and Sockeyes deluge the river along with the Kings. This provided for a large sustainable harvest for the peoples of this area. The Good News is best known for the incredible run of Silver Salmon that start entering the river towards the end of July and continue long into September. Jason was sure they would come back with plenty of fish to smoke, can and share with the others of his town. How proud he would be to give some smoked salmon to his friend Shelly. Silvers are the ideal fly rod salmon, and they will aggressively eat surface flies. Jason had researched this place; the fish were in big trouble. They would not be able to escape his flies and lures. He was going "Hookin'" for fish and they were going in his freezer.

As the plane swung further east, the western end of the Alaska Range came into view. "Wow", he said to himself, his eyes getting bigger.

Big Bill chuckled as Jason pressed his nose against the cold glass. Unlike the Coastal Mountains, the Alaska Range was incredibly vast, jagged, rugged and majestic. The range fought against the expansive blue skies and boasted of its ancient glaciers. Mossy yellow slopes rose to lofty heights, then bled into the darkened summits and snowcapped peaks. The range forms an east-west arc; its center is the most northern part and then bending to the southwest, towards the Alaska Peninsula and southeast into the coastal ranges and Jason's home. The mountains act as a high barrier to the flow of moist air from the Gulf of Alaska up towards the interior, and thus, the area has some of the harshest weather in the world. The heavy snowfall also contributes to a number of rivers of ice. Some of these glaciers he knew: the Cantwell, Castner, Black Rapids, Susitna, and Yanert.

Jason was picturing the glaciers, slowly ever pushing towards the Bearing Sea, when all of a sudden the plane shook and dropped. Bo whined as he was thrown foreword against the front seats. The dog was thrashing and trying to get back on his four feet. The plane now pitched up and poor Bo was thrown back against the gear. Bill was actively trying to level the plane out as it jerked and rolled in the turbulent wind. Jason tightened his belt and gripped his seat. Glancing over at the pilot he could see the man thinking and working his aircraft. The pilot checked on the boy out of the corner of his eye and gave him an uneasy smile, trying to tell him not to worry but soon the Cessna fell. Poor Bo bounced off the ceiling and the belt tightened around Jason pinning him to his seat. Bill had to turn the nose down into a dive and muttered under his breath as they began to fall. He had to level out the wings because the plane had banked left as it fell. The pilot was fighting the wind, the plane and his own fear as it nosed down beginning to spin in, it was hurtling towards the dark land below. Jason closed his eyes and tried to hold down his fear. When he opened them again all he could see was the land rushing up to meet him.

About the Author

Alistair Harden lives in the Interior of Alaska with his loving wife and their dog Brandy.

He came to Alaska in 1989 and has lived all over the state. He now resides in the Interior of Alaska out beyond the power lines. He has made good friends with many Athabaskans and still hunts and fishes with them to this day. Mr. Harden now lives off-grid with a few solar panels, hauls his own water, enjoys gardening, writing and the life of an Alaskan.

With a love for outdoors and the great state of Alaska he has used his knowledge and experience to write about a young boy and his dog Bo. He wishes to encourage the young of Alaska to live life without prejudice and fear. This is his first book in a series that he hopes will teach, entertain and encourage the youth of the world while giving a glimpse into the rural lives of modern Alaskan's.

For other titles from
Alaska Dreams Publishing
please visit
www.alaskadp.com

If you'd like to be notified when the next book in the Jason and Bo series is released, please sign up for the ADP mailing list at:
http://www.alaskadp.com/signup.html

Follow us on:
Twitter: @alaskadp
Facebook: **https://www.facebook.com/alaskadp**

www.ingramcontent.com/pod-product-compliance
Lightning Source LLC
Chambersburg PA
CBHW020648130626
46552CB00003B/1447